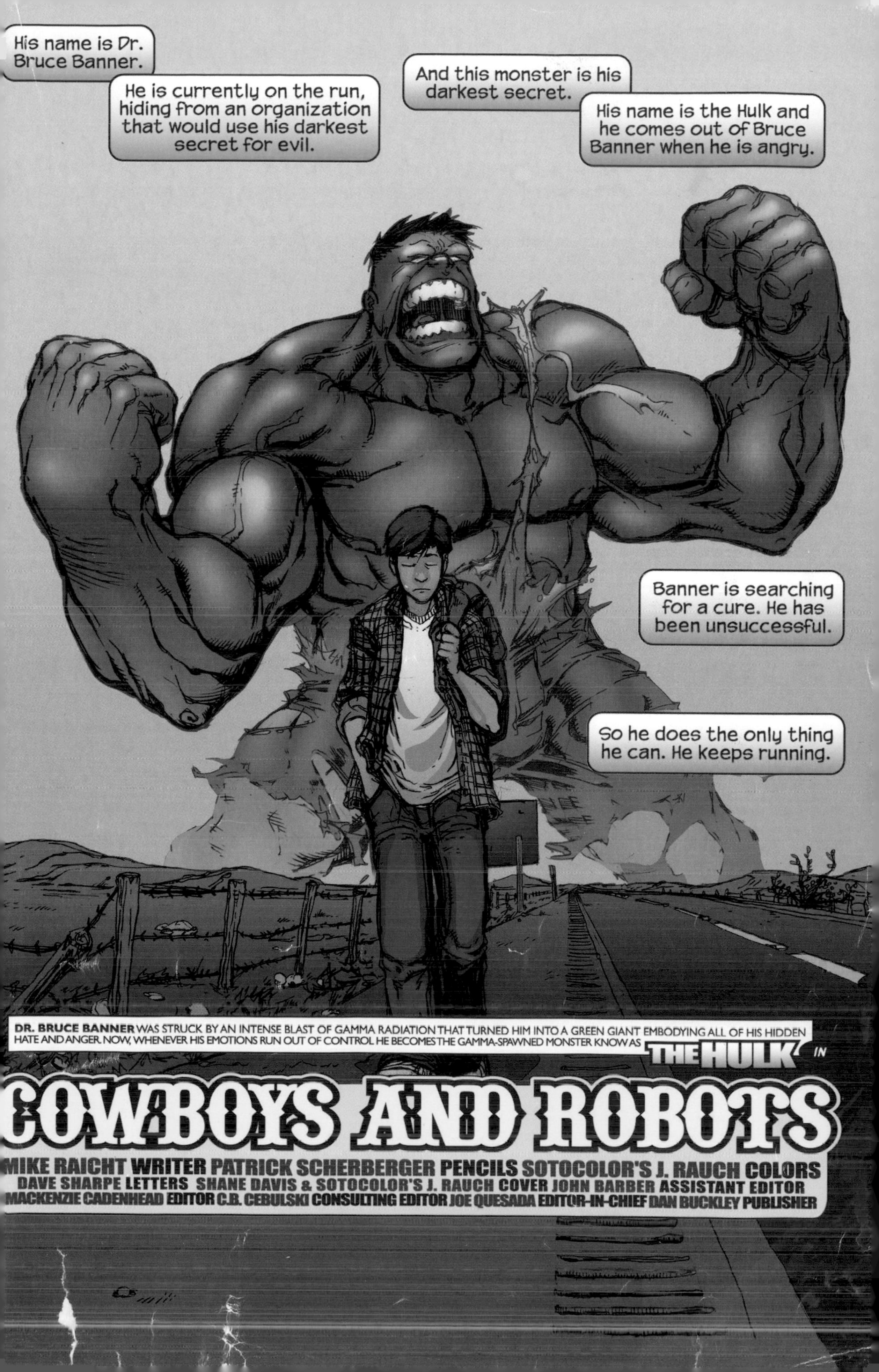

His name is Dr. Bruce Banner.
He is currently on the run, hiding from an organization that would use his darkest secret for evil.
And this monster is his darkest secret.
His name is the Hulk and he comes out of Bruce Banner when he is angry.
Banner is searching for a cure. He has been unsuccessful.
So he does the only thing he can. He keeps running.
DR. BRUCE BANNER WAS STRUCK BY AN INTENSE BLAST OF GAMMA RADIATION THAT TURNED HIM INTO A GREEN GIANT EMBODYING ALL OF HIS HIDDEN HATE AND ANGER. NOW, WHENEVER HIS EMOTIONS RUN OUT OF CONTROL HE BECOMES THE GAMMA-SPAWNED MONSTER KNOW AS THE HULK IN
COWBOYS AND ROBOTS
MIKE RAICHT WRITER PATRICK SCHERBERGER PENCILS SOTOCOLOR'S J. RAUCH COLORS
DAVE SHARPE LETTERS SHANE DAVIS & SOTOCOLOR'S J. RAUCH COVER JOHN BARBER ASSISTANT EDITOR
MACKENZIE CADENHEAD EDITOR C.B. CEBULSKI CONSULTING EDITOR JOE QUESADA EDITOR-IN-CHIEF DAN BUCKLEY PUBLISHER

VISIT US AT

www.abdopub.com

Spotlight, a division of ABDO Publishing Company Inc., is the school and library distributor of the Marvel Entertainment books.

Library bound edition © 2006

Library of Congress Cataloging-in-Publication Data

Raicht, Mike.
    The Hulk in cowboys and robots / Mike Raicht, writer ; Patrick Scherberger, pencils ; J. Rauch, colors ; Dave Sharpe, letters ; Shane Davis & J. Rauch, cover.
        p. cm.
    "Marvel age"—Cover.
    Revision of a Dec. 2004 issue of Incredible Hulk.
    ISBN 1-59961-044-2
    1. Graphic novels. I. Title: Cowboys and robots. II. Incredible Hulk (New York, N.Y. : 1999)
III. Scherberger, Patrick. IV. Title.

PN6728.H8R344 2006
741.5'973—dc22

2005057560

All Spotlight books are reinforced library binding
and manufactured in the United States of America

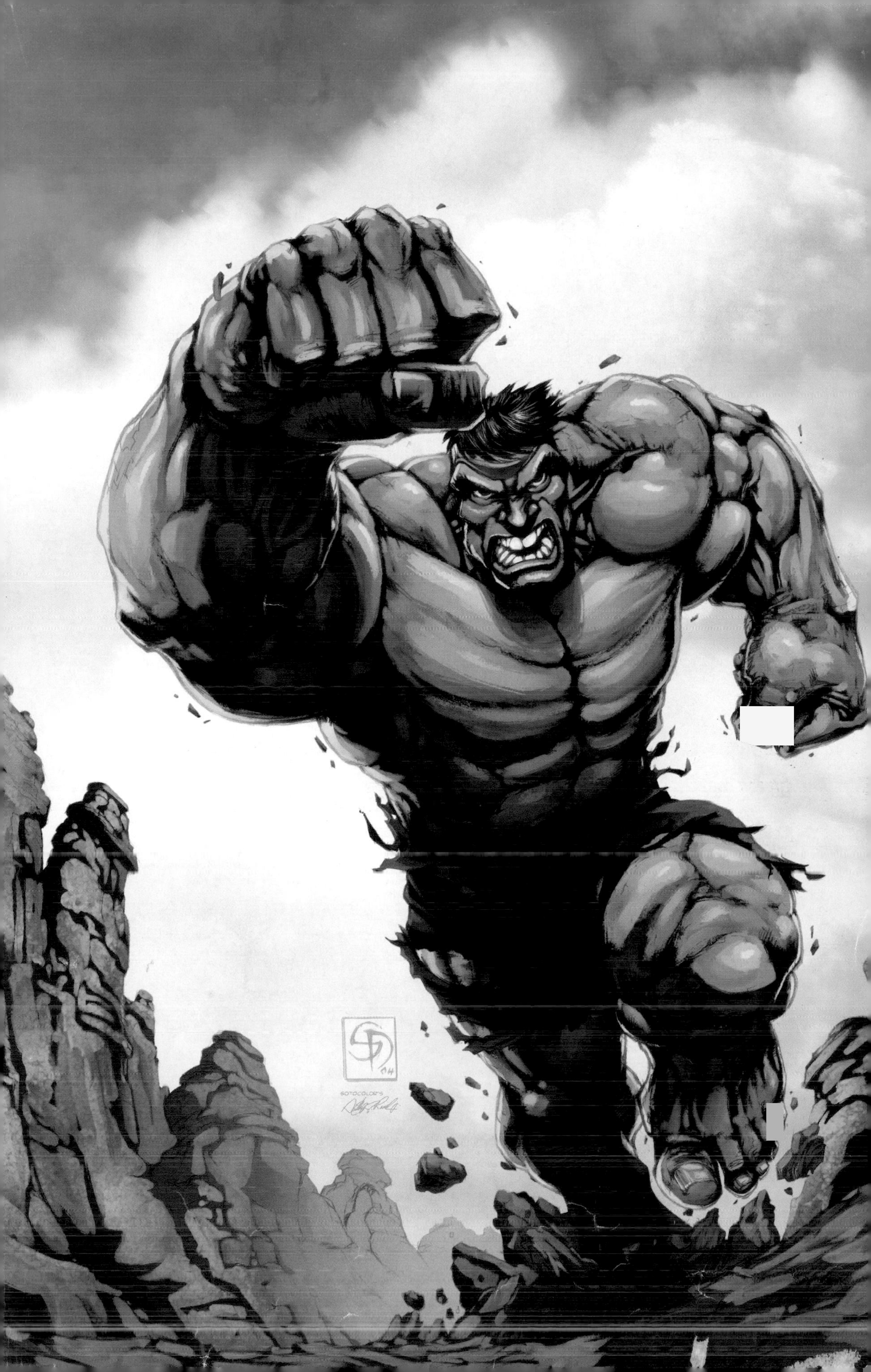
'04
SOTOCOLOR'S

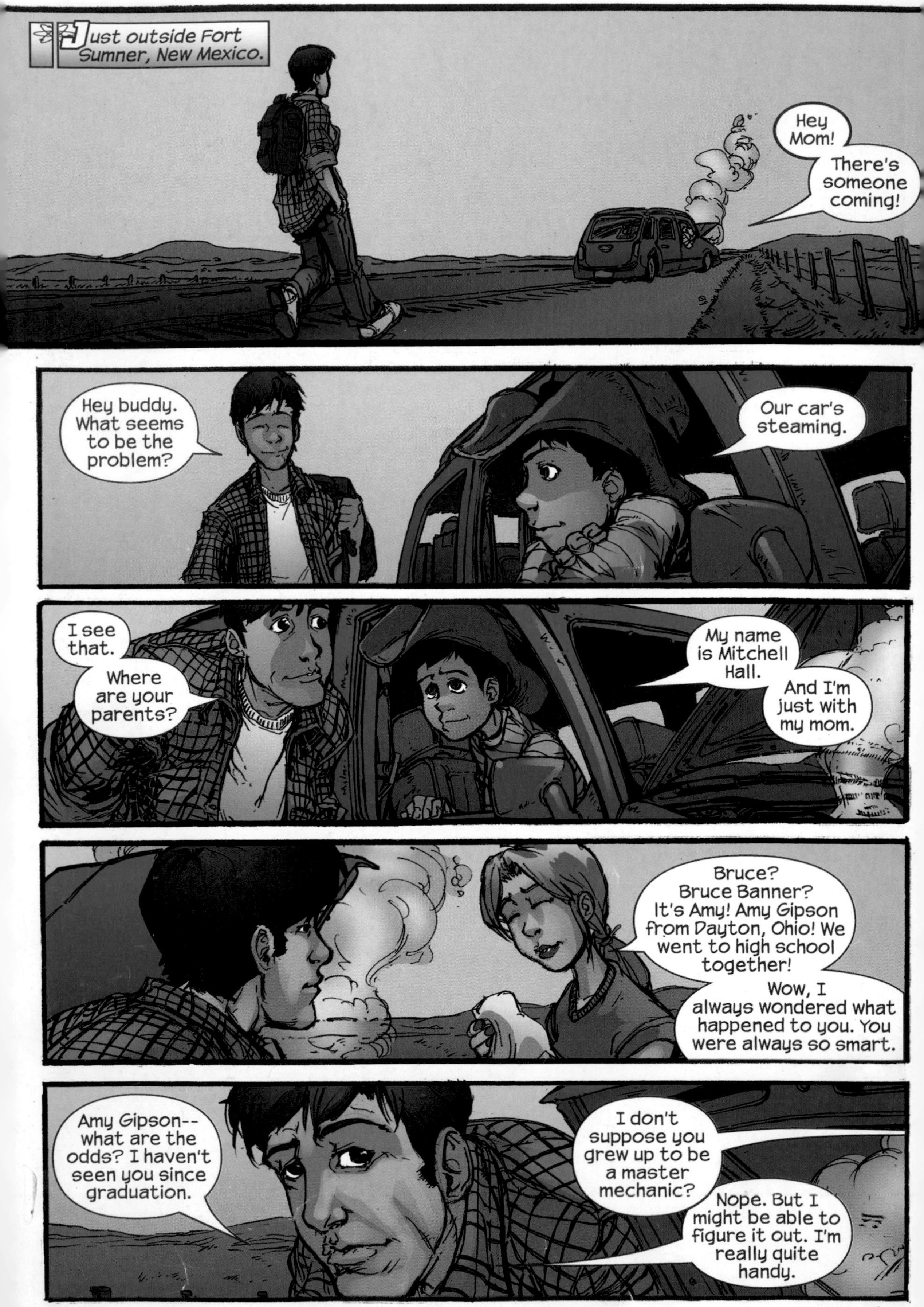
Just outside Fort Sumner, New Mexico.
Hey Mom!
There's someone coming!
Hey buddy. What seems to be the problem?
Our car's steaming.
I see that.
Where are your parents?
My name is Mitchell Hall.
And I'm just with my mom.
Bruce? Bruce Banner? It's Amy! Amy Gipson from Dayton, Ohio! We went to high school together!
Wow, I always wondered what happened to you. You were always so smart.
Amy Gipson-- what are the odds? I haven't seen you since graduation.
I don't suppose you grew up to be a master mechanic?
Nope. But I might be able to figure it out. I'm really quite handy.

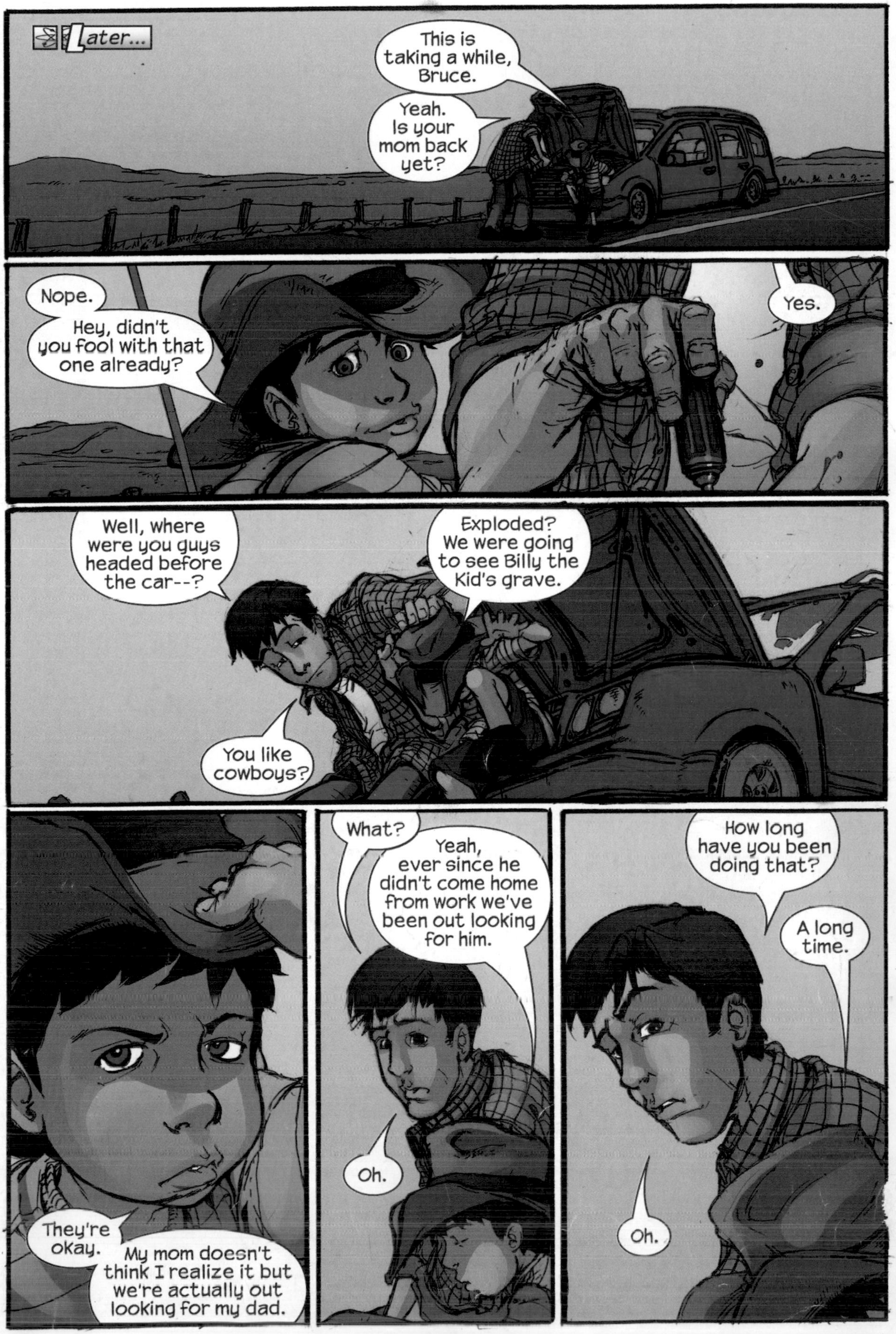
Later...
This is taking a while, Bruce.
Yeah. Is your mom back yet?
Nope.
Hey, didn't you fool with that one already?
Yes.
Well, where were you guys headed before the car--?
Exploded? We were going to see Billy the Kid's grave.
You like cowboys?
They're okay.
My mom doesn't think I realize it but we're actually out looking for my dad.
What?
Yeah, ever since he didn't come home from work we've been out looking for him.
Oh.
How long have you been doing that?
A long time.
Oh.

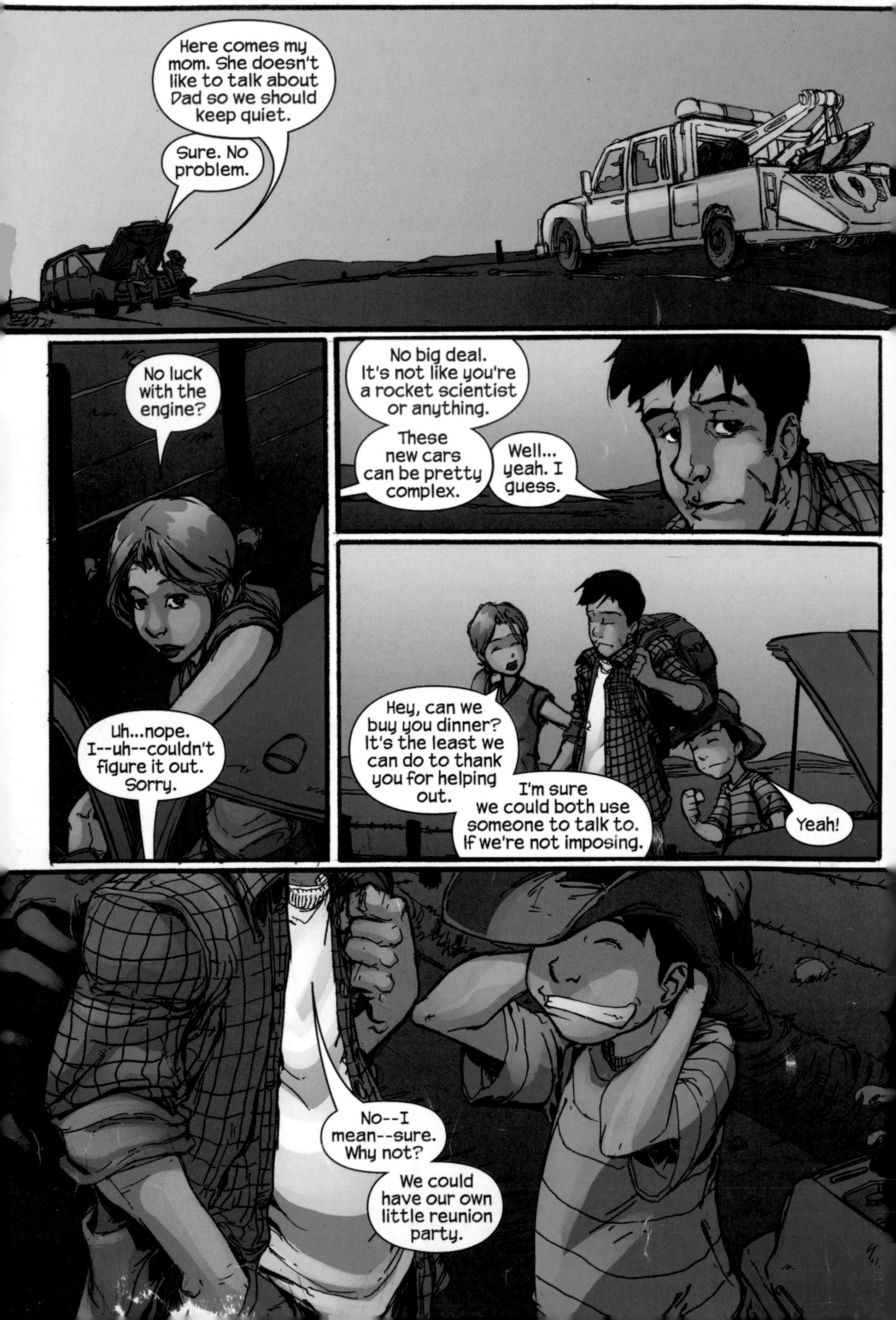
Here comes my mom. She doesn't like to talk about Dad so we should keep quiet.
Sure. No problem.
No luck with the engine?
Uh...nope. I--uh--couldn't figure it out. Sorry.
No big deal. It's not like you're a rocket scientist or anything.
These new cars can be pretty complex.
Well... yeah. I guess.
Hey, can we buy you dinner? It's the least we can do to thank you for helping out.
I'm sure we could both use someone to talk to. If we're not imposing.
Yeah!
No--I mean--sure. Why not?
We could have our own little reunion party.

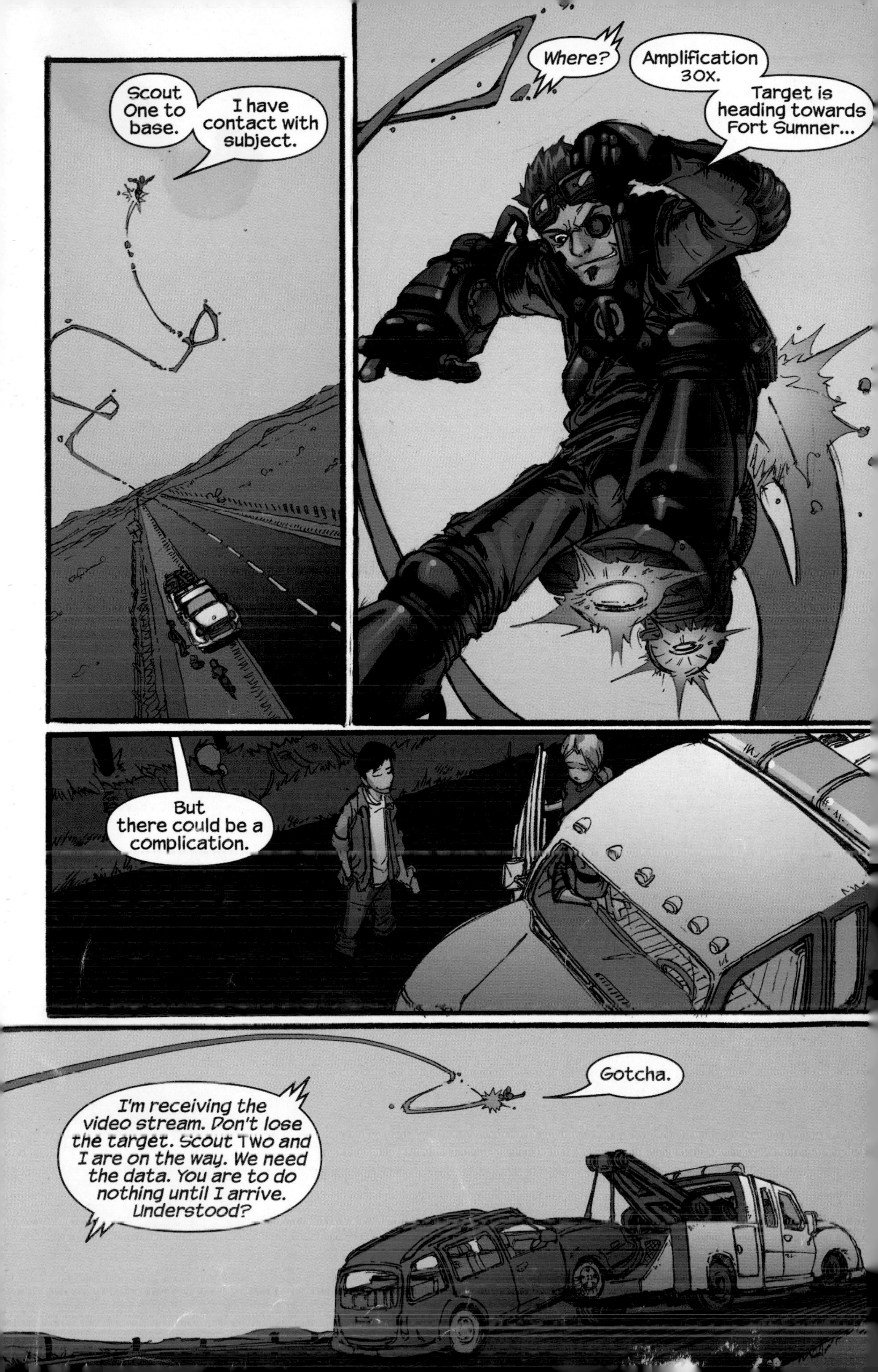
Scout One to base.
I have contact with subject.
Where?
Amplification 30X.
Target is heading towards Fort Sumner...
But there could be a complication.
Gotcha.
I'm receiving the video stream. Don't lose the target. Scout Two and I are on the way. We need the data. You are to do nothing until I arrive. Understood?

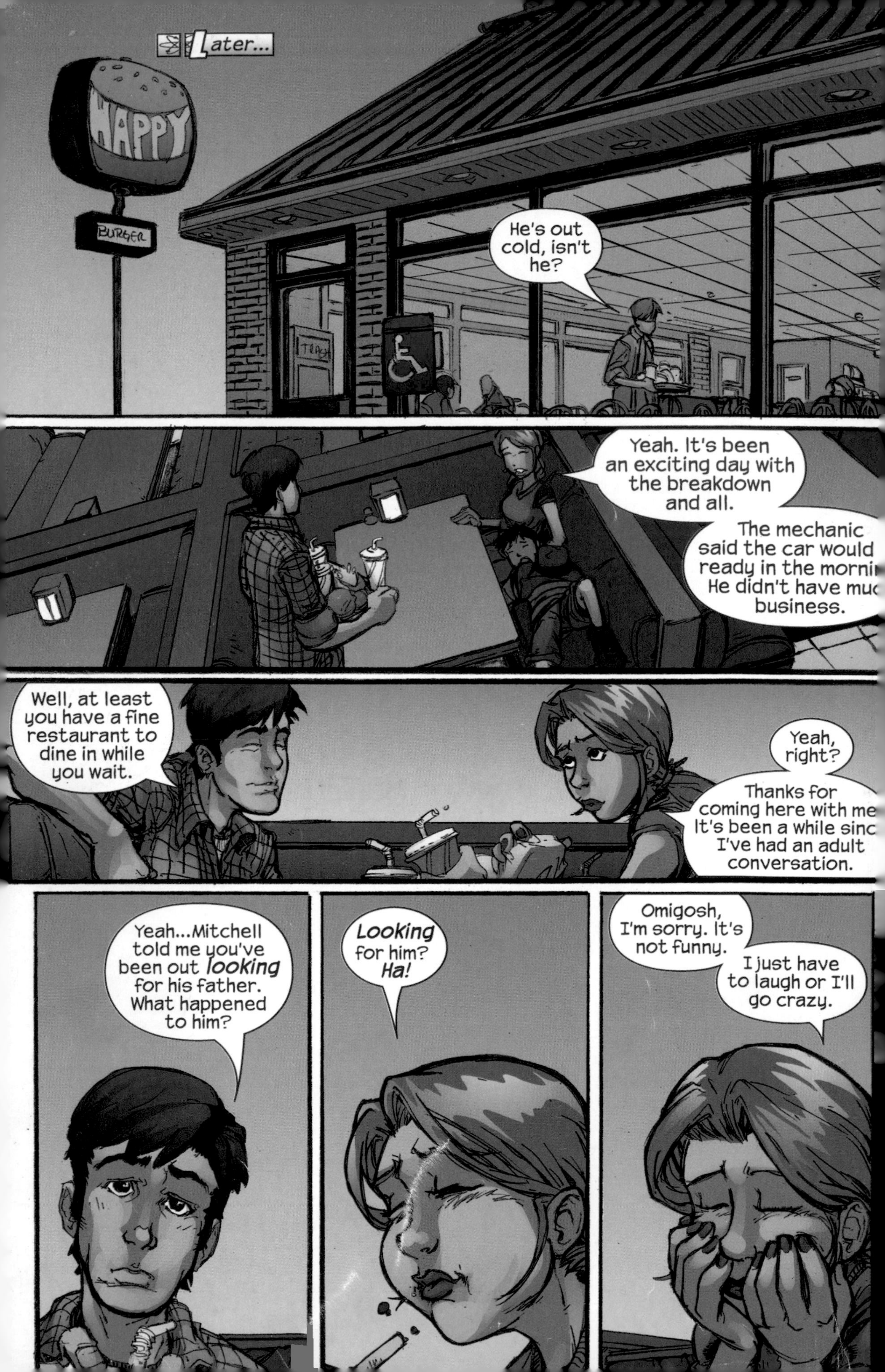
Later...
HAPPY
BURGER
TRASH
He's out cold, isn't he?
Yeah. It's been an exciting day with the breakdown and all.
The mechanic said the car would ready in the morni
He didn't have muc business.
Well, at least you have a fine restaurant to dine in while you wait.
Yeah, right?
Thanks for coming here with me
It's been a while sinc I've had an adult conversation.
Yeah...Mitchell told me you've been out *looking* for his father. What happened to him?
Looking for him? ***Ha!***
Omigosh, I'm sorry. It's not funny.
I just have to laugh or I'll go crazy.

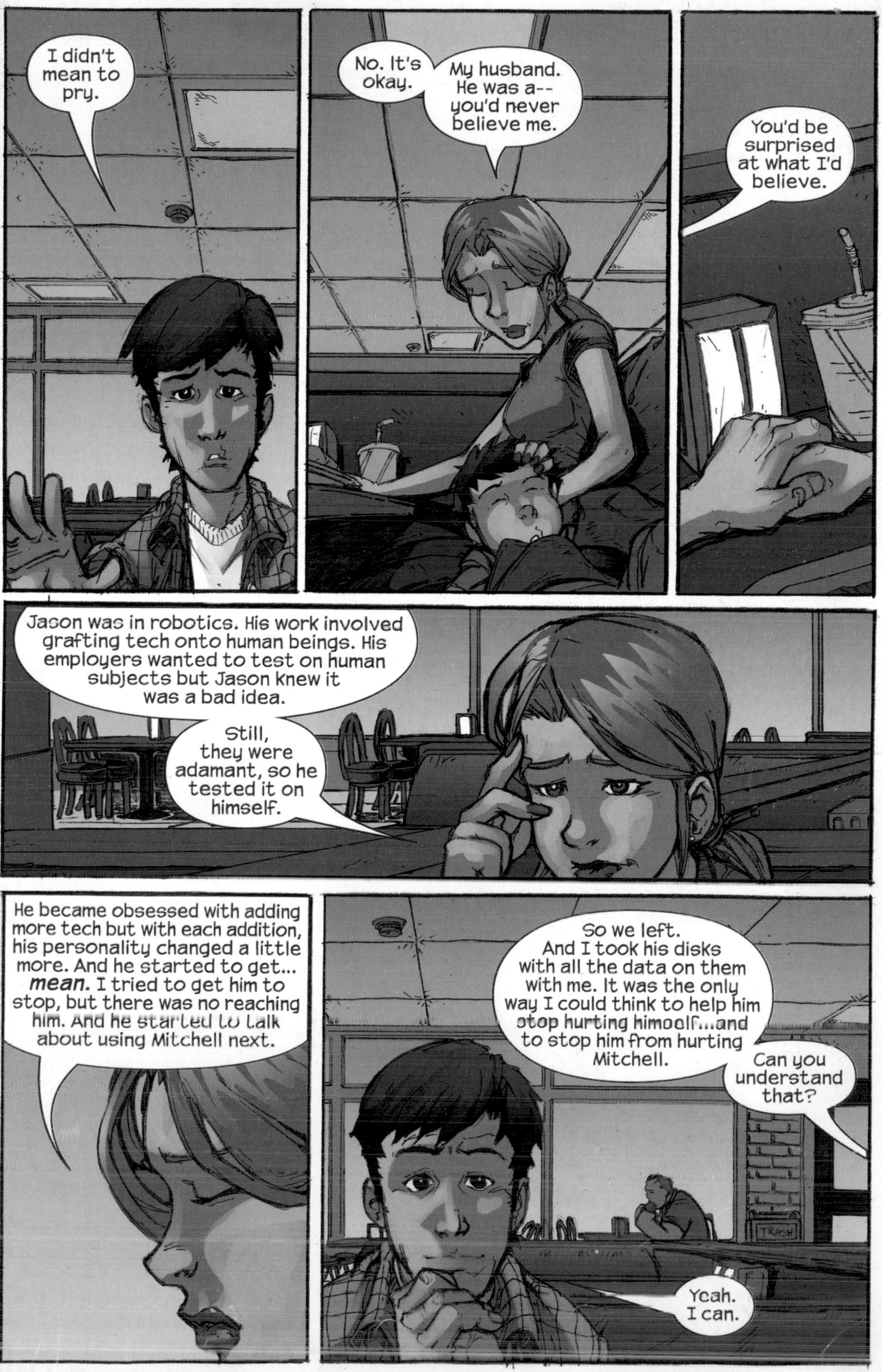
I didn't mean to pry.
No. It's okay.
My husband. He was a-- you'd never believe me.
You'd be surprised at what I'd believe.
Jason was in robotics. His work involved grafting tech onto human beings. His employers wanted to test on human subjects but Jason knew it was a bad idea.
Still, they were adamant, so he tested it on himself.
He became obsessed with adding more tech but with each addition, his personality changed a little more. And he started to get... *mean.* I tried to get him to stop, but there was no reaching him. And he started to talk about using Mitchell next.
So we left. And I took his disks with all the data on them with me. It was the only way I could think to help him stop hurting himself...and to stop him from hurting Mitchell.
Can you understand that?
TRASH
Yeah. I can.

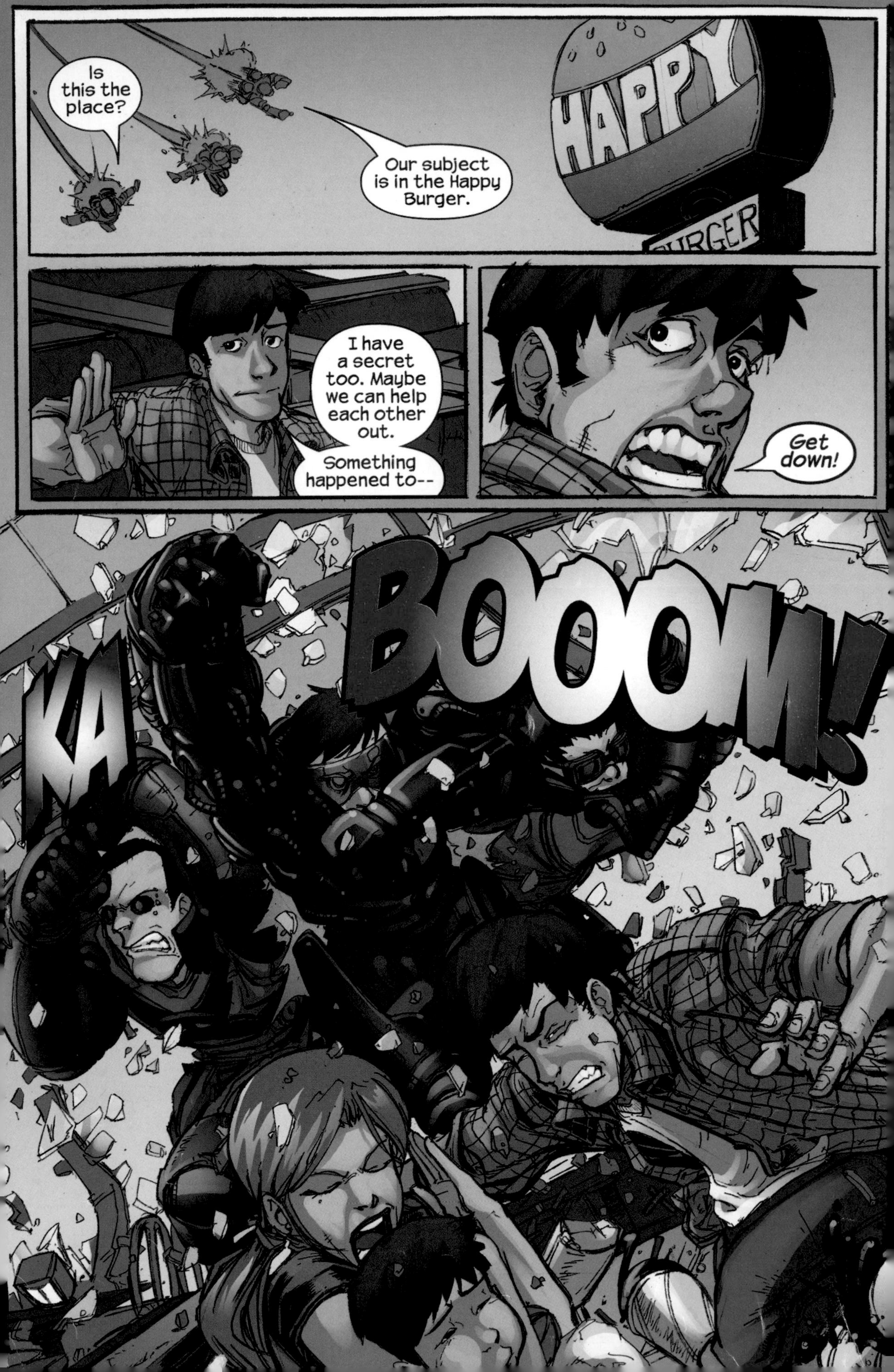
Is this the place?
Our subject is in the Happy Burger.
HAPPY
BURGER
I have a secret too. Maybe we can help each other out.
Something happened to--
Get down!
KA
BOOOM!

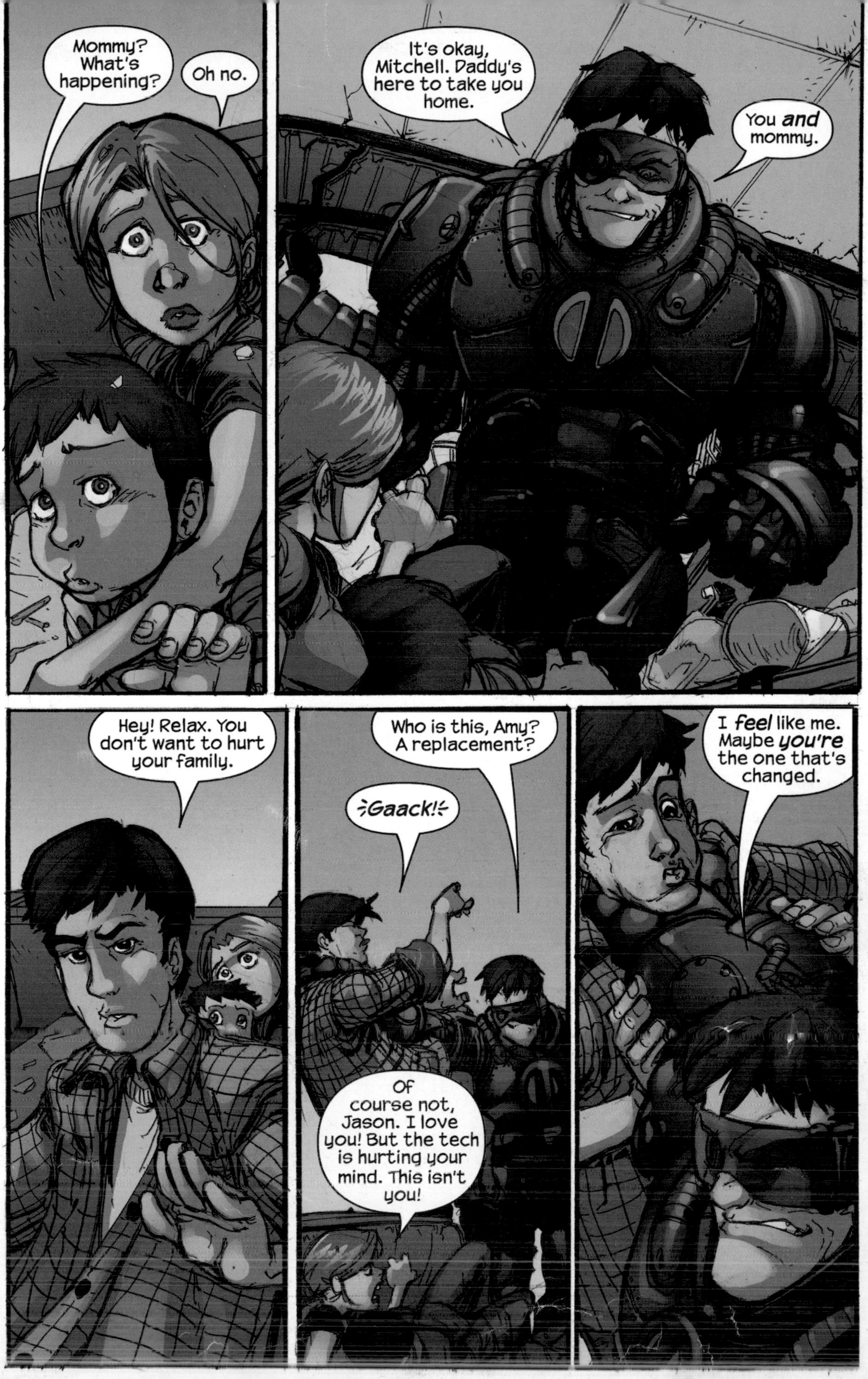
Mommy? What's happening?
Oh no.
It's okay, Mitchell. Daddy's here to take you home.
You *and* mommy.
Hey! Relax. You don't want to hurt your family.
Who is this, Amy? A replacement?
Gaack!
Of course not, Jason. I love you! But the tech is hurting your mind. This isn't you!
I *feel* like me. Maybe *you're* the one that's changed.

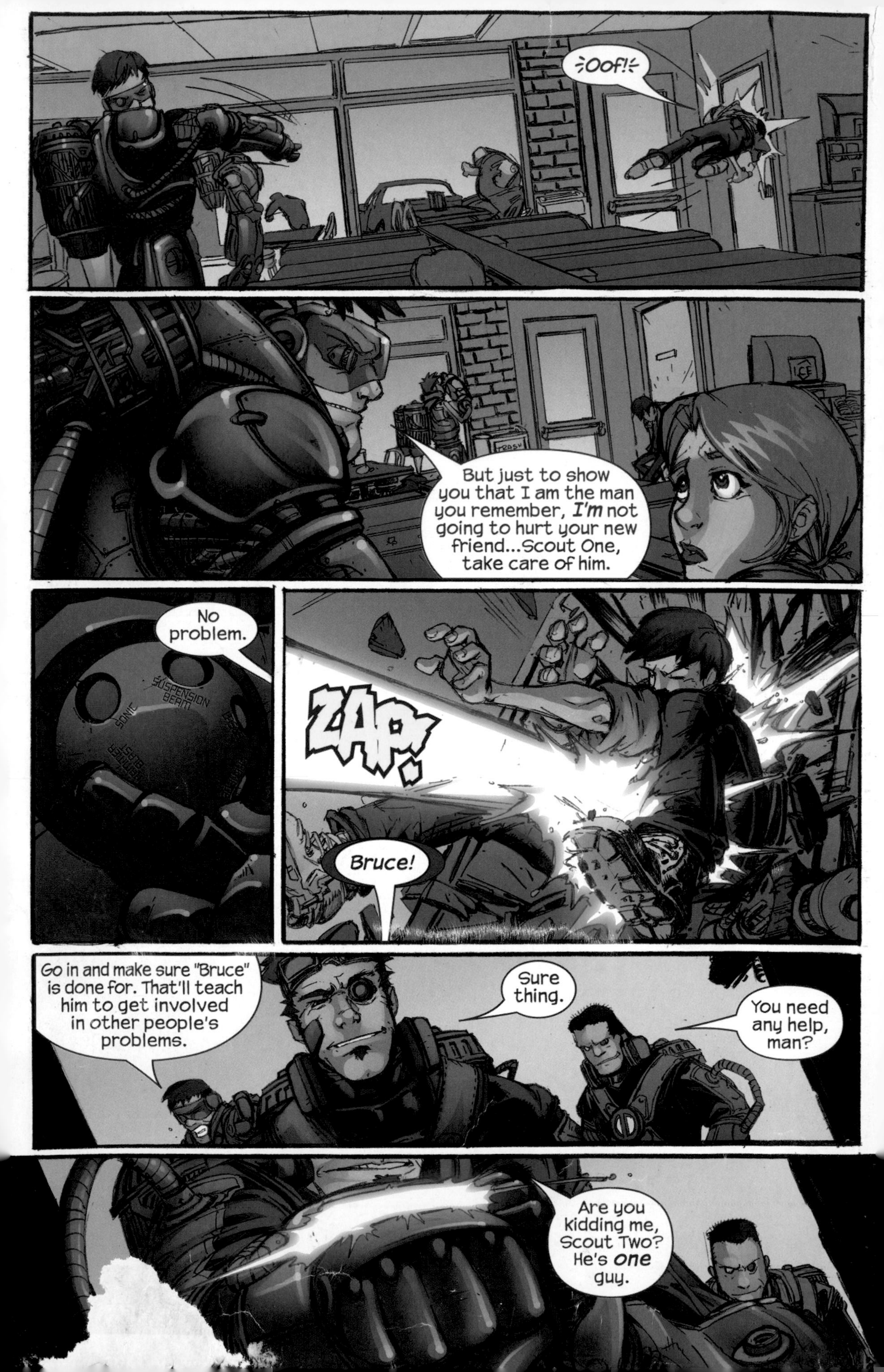
Oof!
But just to show you that I am the man you remember, *I'm* not going to hurt your new friend...Scout One, take care of him.
No problem.
SUSPENSION BEAM
SONIC
ZAP!
Bruce!
Go in and make sure "Bruce" is done for. That'll teach him to get involved in other people's problems.
Sure thing.
You need any help, man?
Are you kidding me, Scout Two? He's *one* guy.

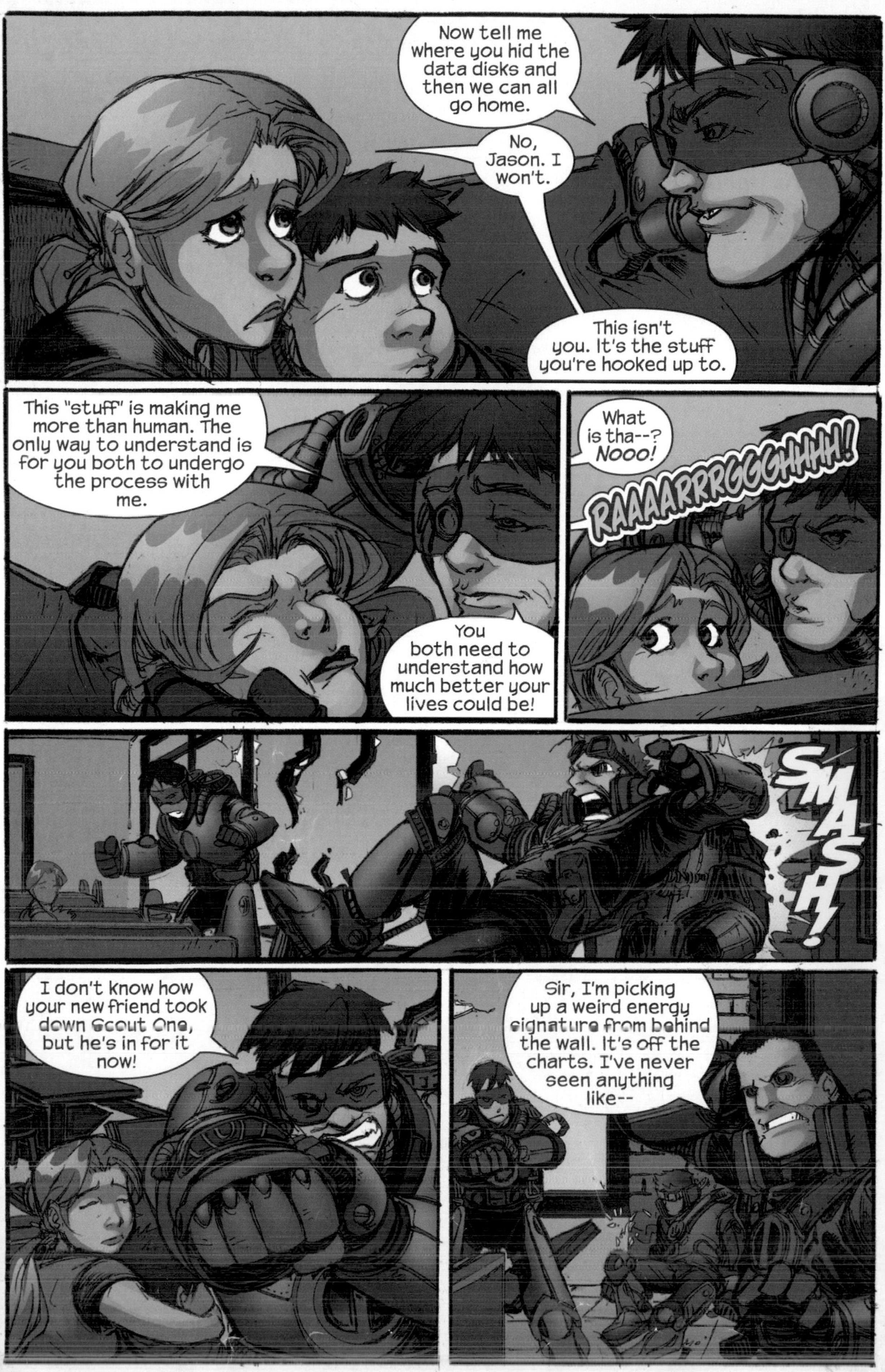
Now tell me where you hid the data disks and then we can all go home.
No, Jason. I won't.
This isn't you. It's the stuff you're hooked up to.
This "stuff" is making me more than human. The only way to understand is for you both to undergo the process with me.
You both need to understand how much better your lives could be!
What is tha--? Nooo!
RAAAARRRGGGHHHH!
SMASH!
I don't know how your new friend took down Scout One, but he's in for it now!
Sir, I'm picking up a weird energy signature from behind the wall. It's off the charts. I've never seen anything like--

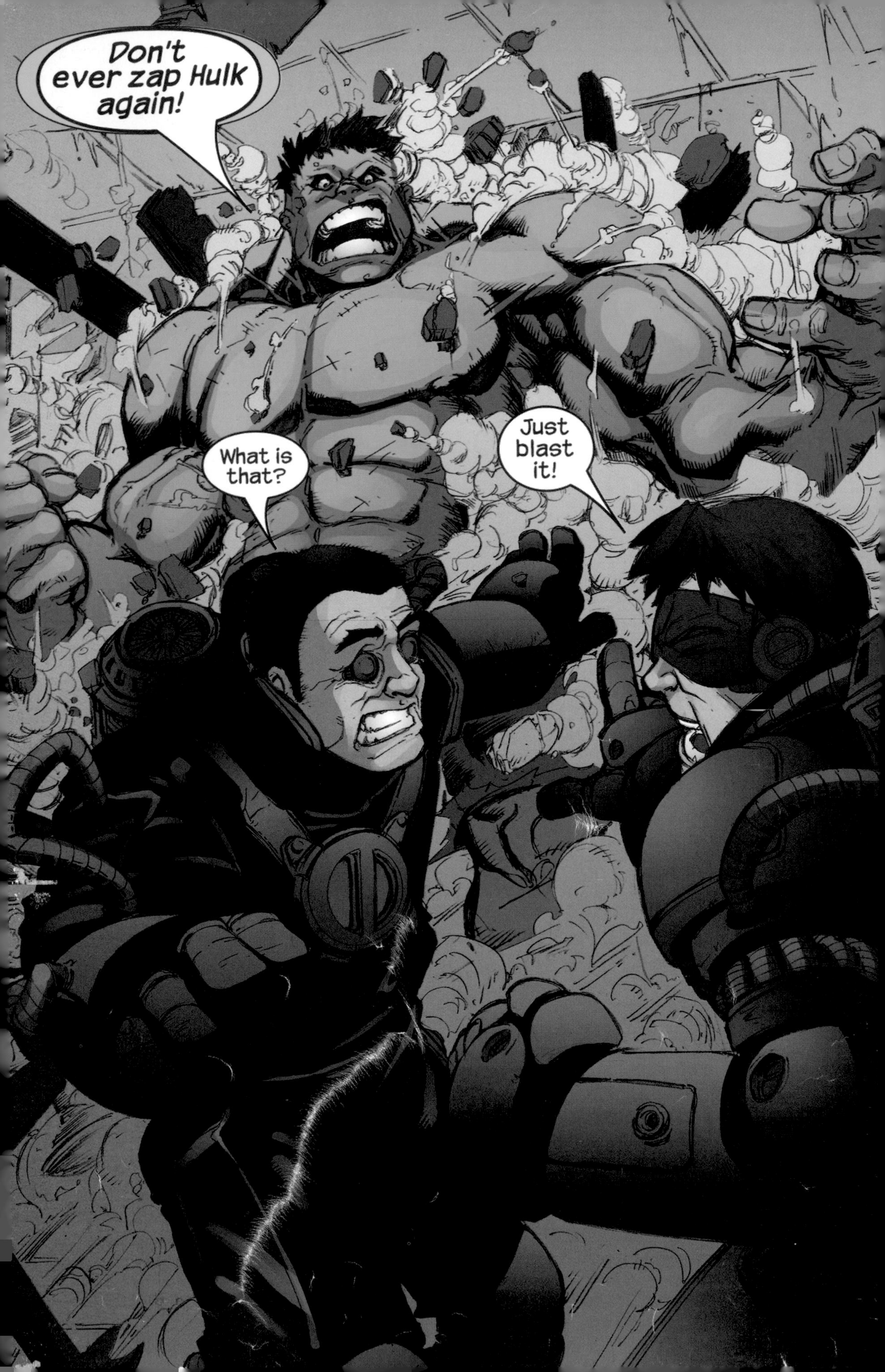
Don't ever zap Hulk again!
What is that?
Just blast it!

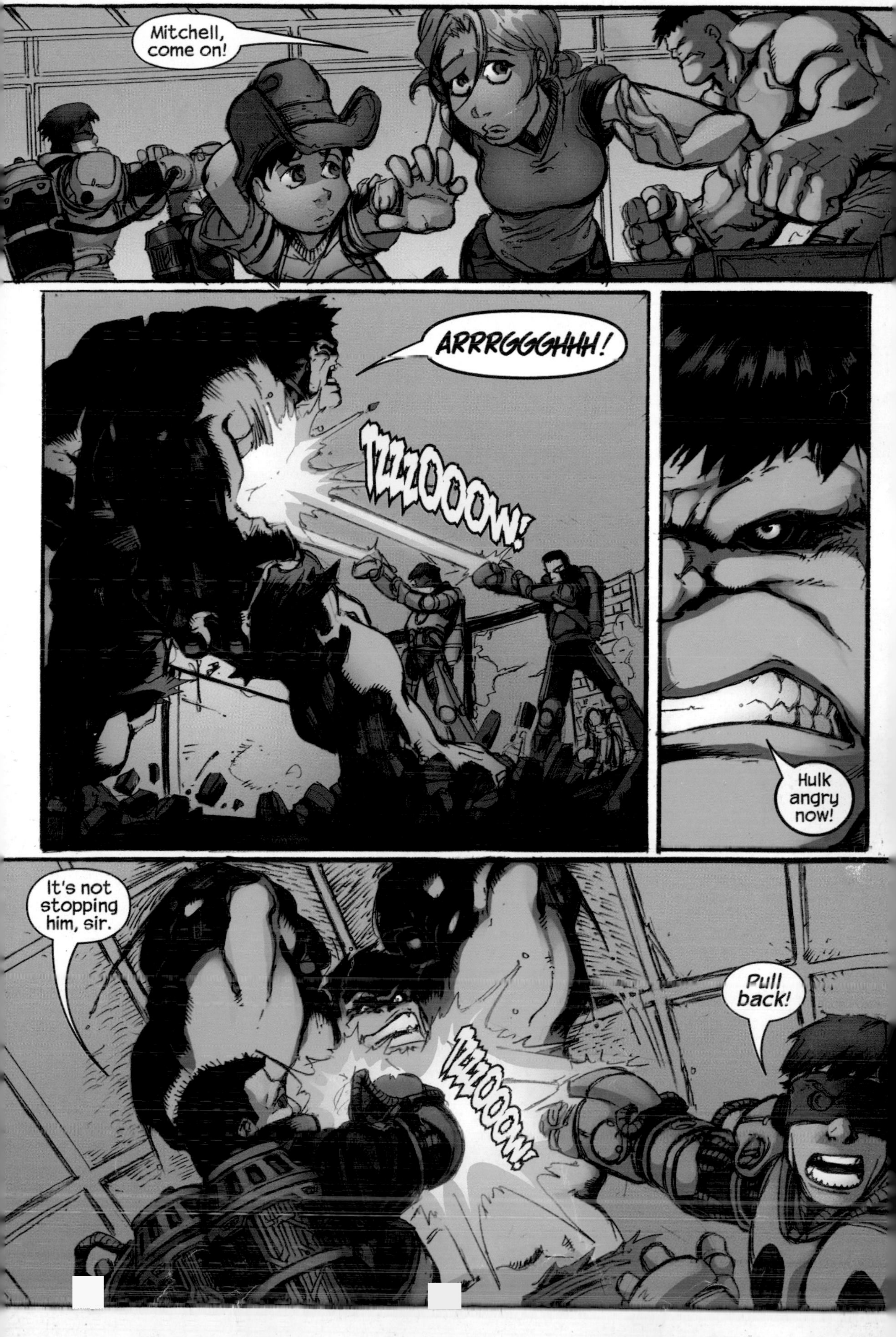
Mitchell, come on!
ARRRGGGHHH!
TZZZOOOW!
Hulk angry now!
It's not stopping him, sir.
Pull back!
TZZZOOOW!

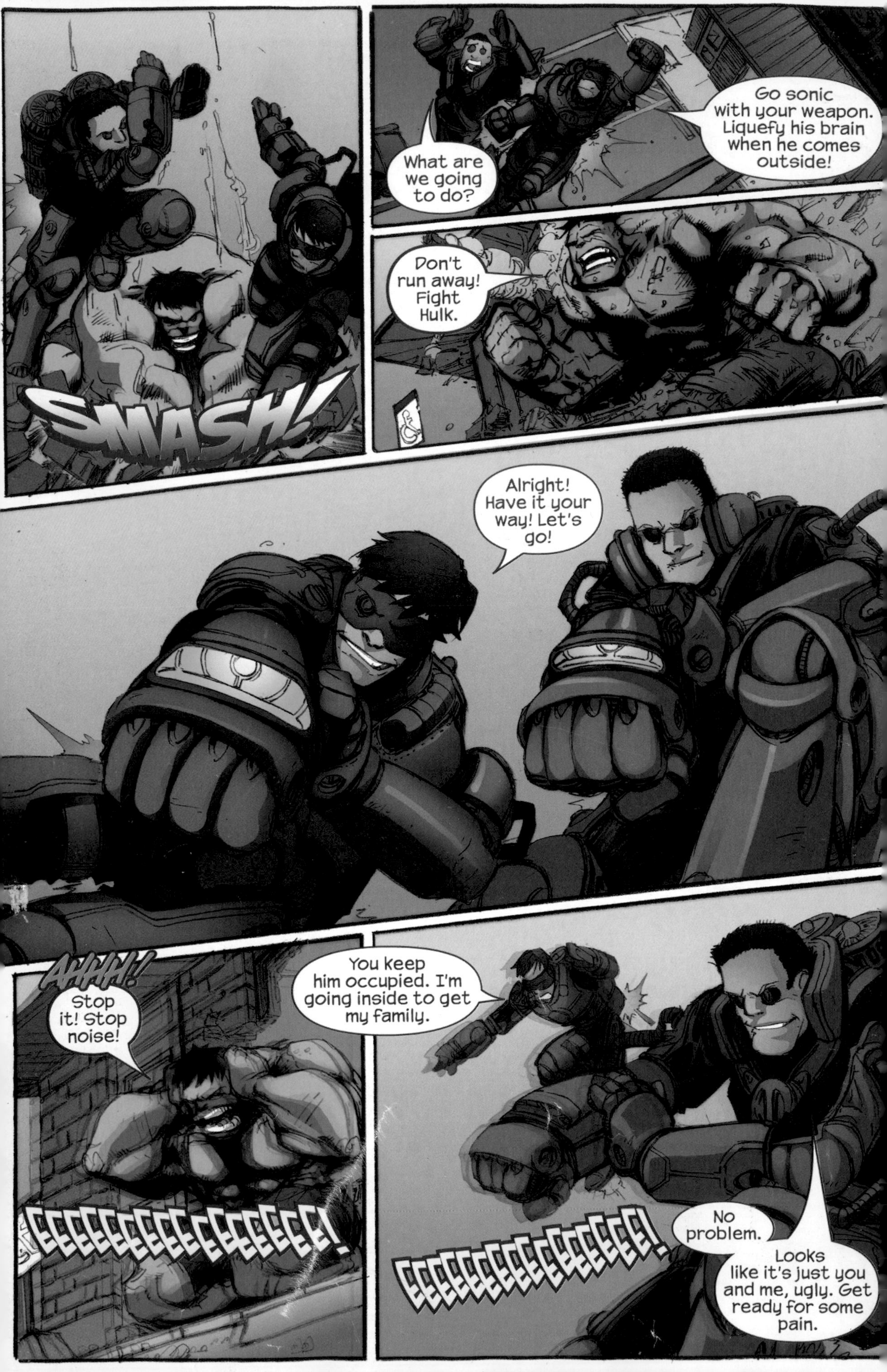
SMASH!
What are we going to do?
Go sonic with your weapon. Liquefy his brain when he comes outside!
Don't run away! Fight Hulk.
Alright! Have it your way! Let's go!
AHHH!
Stop it! Stop noise!
EEEEEEEEEEEEEEEEEEE!
You keep him occupied. I'm going inside to get my family.
EEEEEEEEEEEEEEEEE!
No problem.
Looks like it's just you and me, ugly. Get ready for some pain.

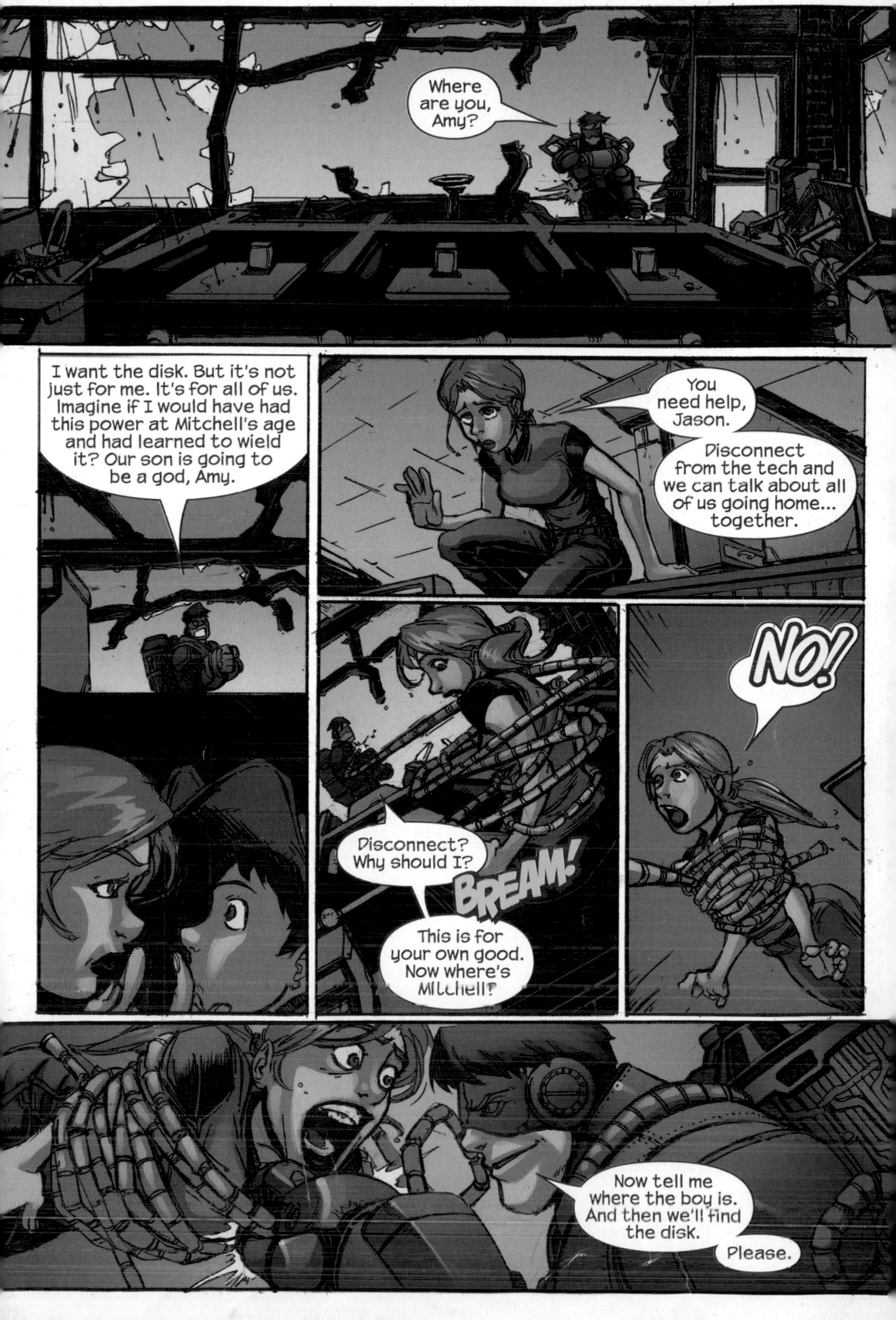

Where are you, Amy?
I want the disk. But it's not just for me. It's for all of us. Imagine if I would have had this power at Mitchell's age and had learned to wield it? Our son is going to be a god, Amy.
You need help, Jason.
Disconnect from the tech and we can talk about all of us going home... together.
Disconnect? Why should I?
BREAM!
This is for your own good. Now where's Mitchell?
NO!
Now tell me where the boy is. And then we'll find the disk.
Please.

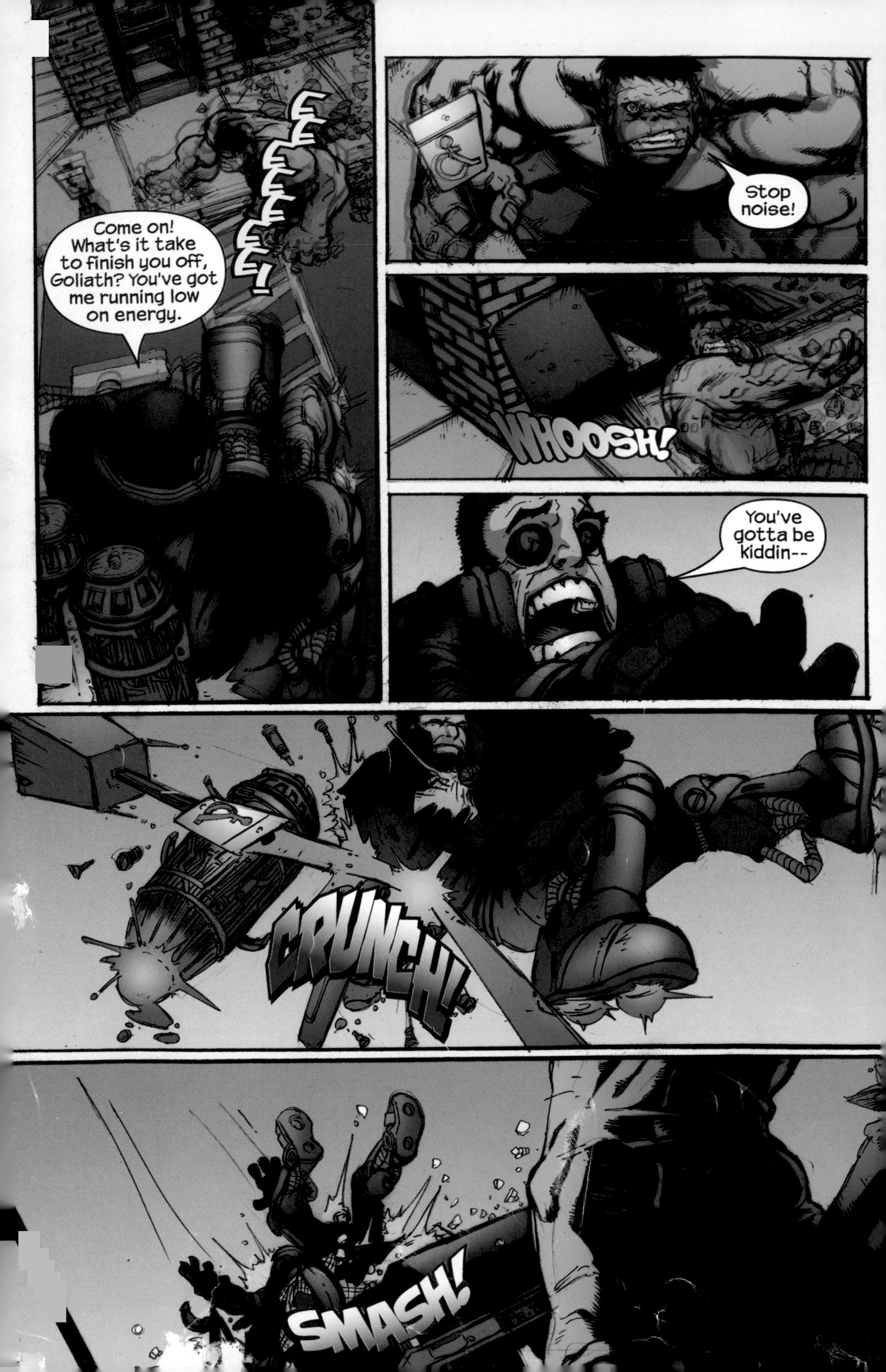
EEEEEEEEE!
Come on! What's it take to finish you off, Goliath? You've got me running low on energy.
Stop noise!
WHOOSH!
You've gotta be kiddin--
CRUNCH!
SMASH!

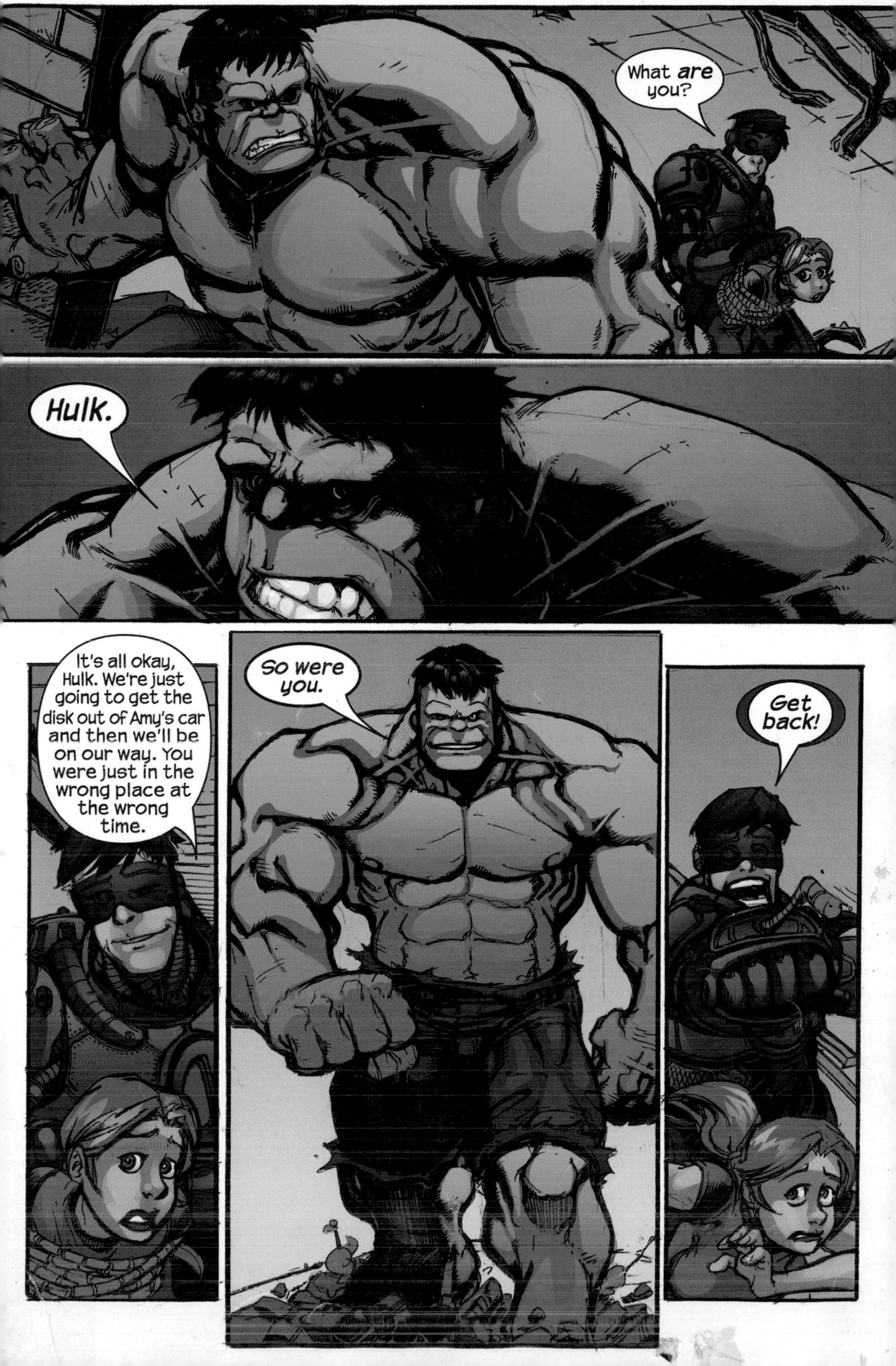
What are you?
Hulk.
It's all okay, Hulk. We're just going to get the disk out of Amy's car and then we'll be on our way. You were just in the wrong place at the wrong time.
So were you.
Get back!

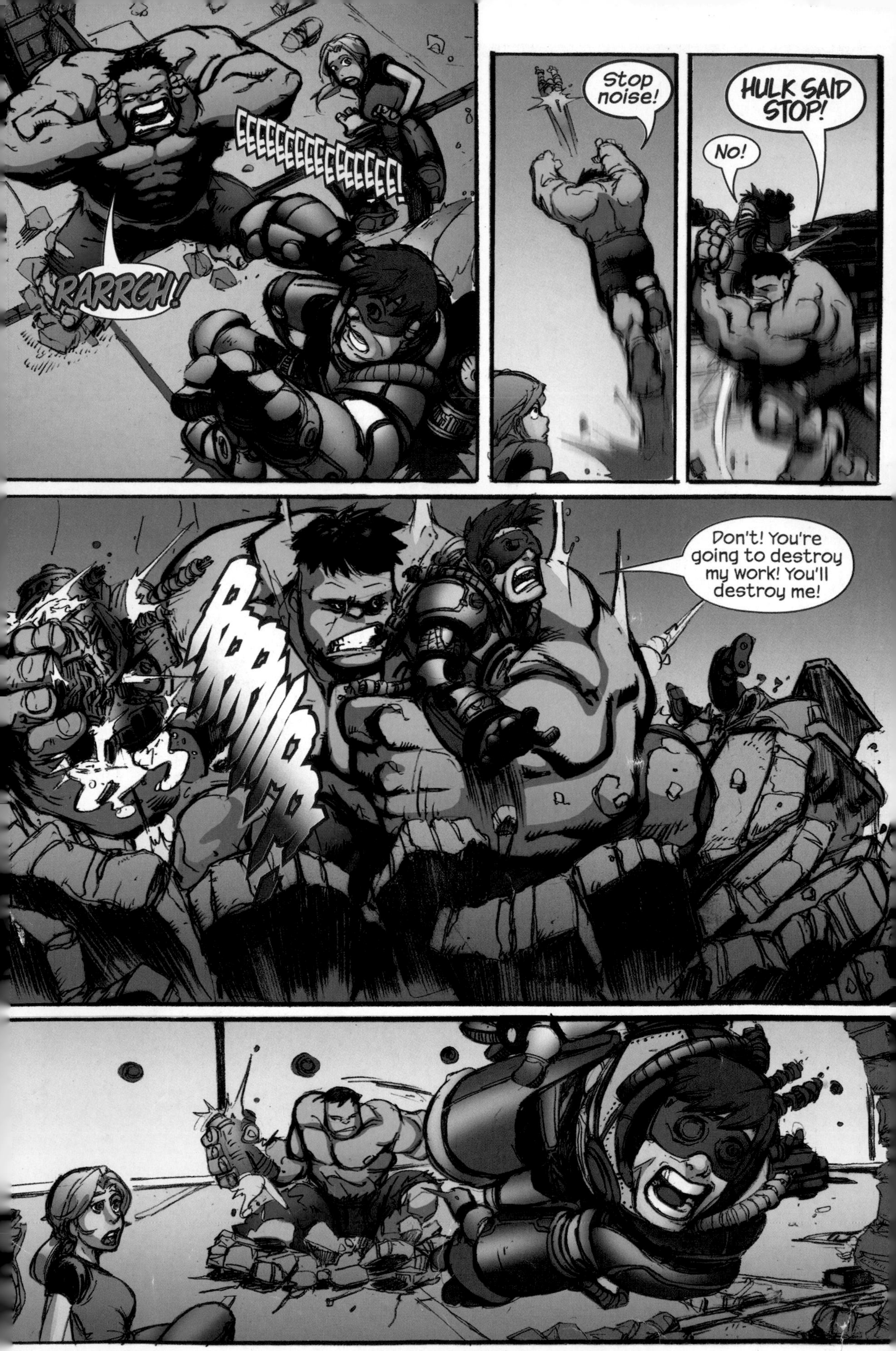
EEEEEEEEEEEEEEEEEEE!
RARRGH!
Stop noise!
HULK SAID STOP!
No!
Don't! You're going to destroy my work! You'll destroy me!

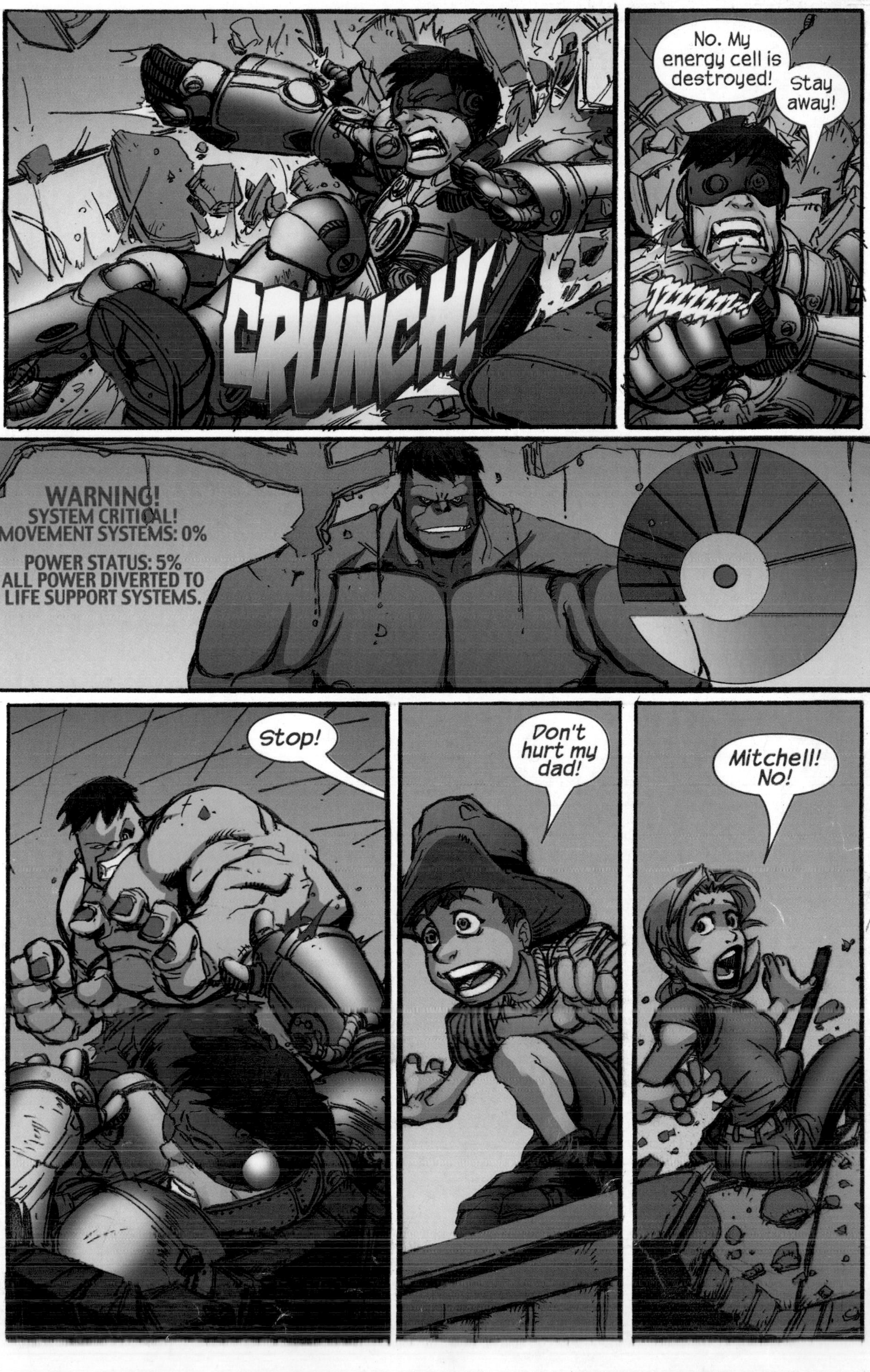
CRUNCH!
No. My energy cell is destroyed!
Stay away!
WARNING!
SYSTEM CRITICAL!
MOVEMENT SYSTEMS: 0%
POWER STATUS: 5%
ALL POWER DIVERTED TO LIFE SUPPORT SYSTEMS.
Stop!
Don't hurt my dad!
Mitchell! No!

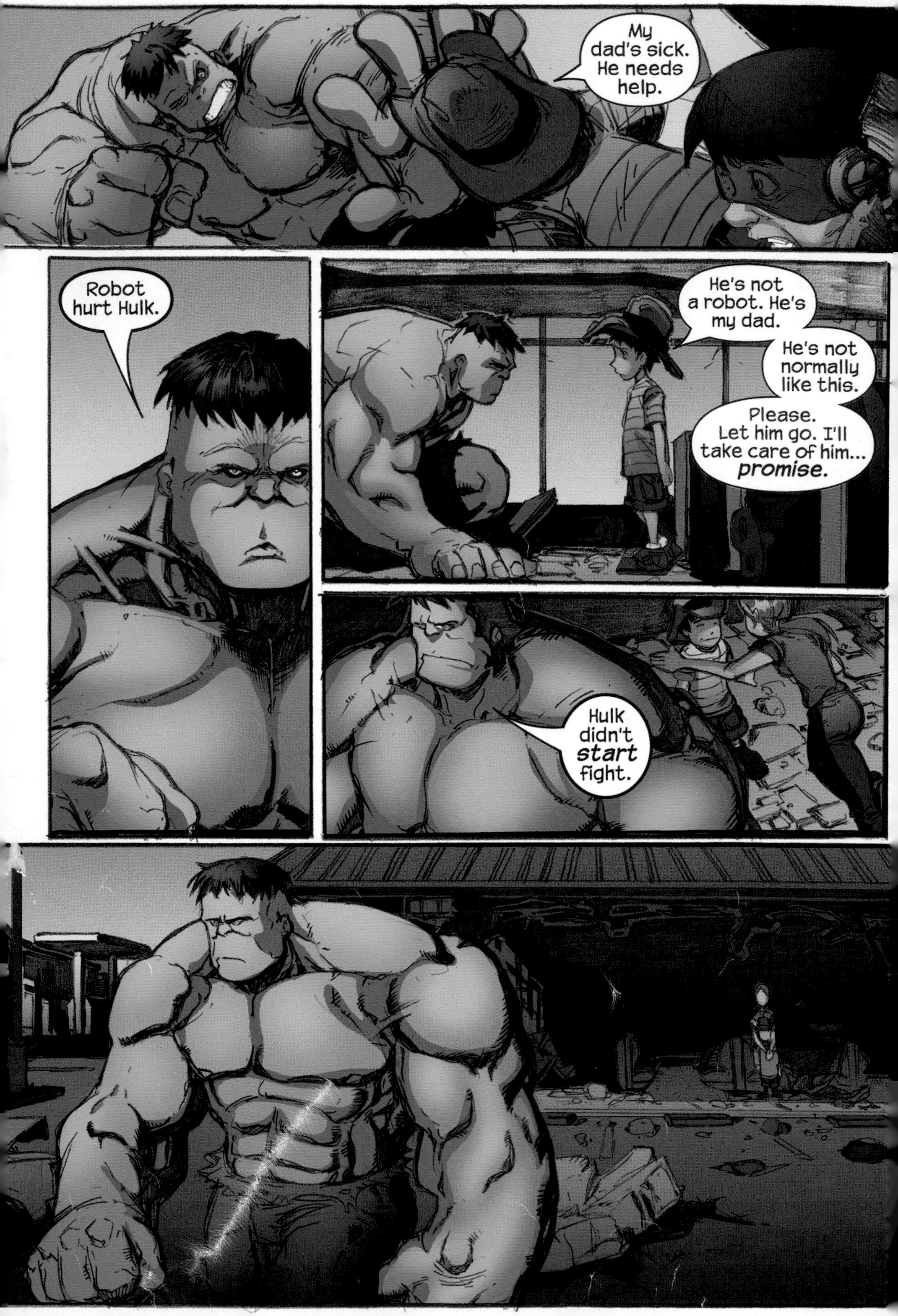
My dad's sick. He needs help.
Robot hurt Hulk.
He's not a robot. He's my dad.
He's not normally like this.
Please. Let him go. I'll take care of him... *promise.*
Hulk didn't *start* fight.

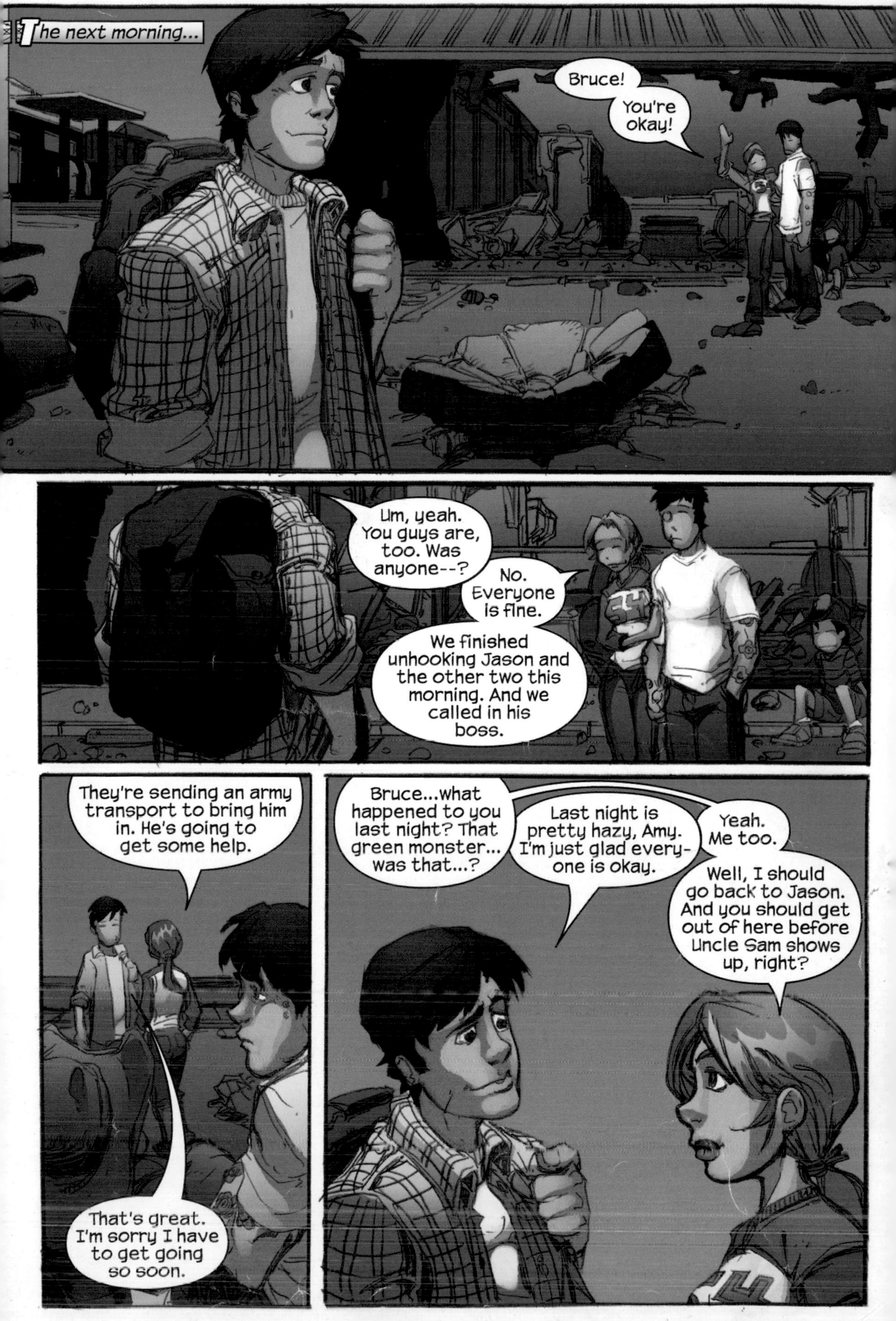
The next morning...
Bruce!
You're okay!
Um, yeah. You guys are, too. Was anyone--?
No. Everyone is fine.
We finished unhooking Jason and the other two this morning. And we called in his boss.
They're sending an army transport to bring him in. He's going to get some help.
That's great. I'm sorry I have to get going so soon.
Bruce...what happened to you last night? That green monster... was that...?
Last night is pretty hazy, Amy. I'm just glad every-one is okay.
Yeah. Me too.
Well, I should go back to Jason. And you should get out of here before Uncle Sam shows up, right?

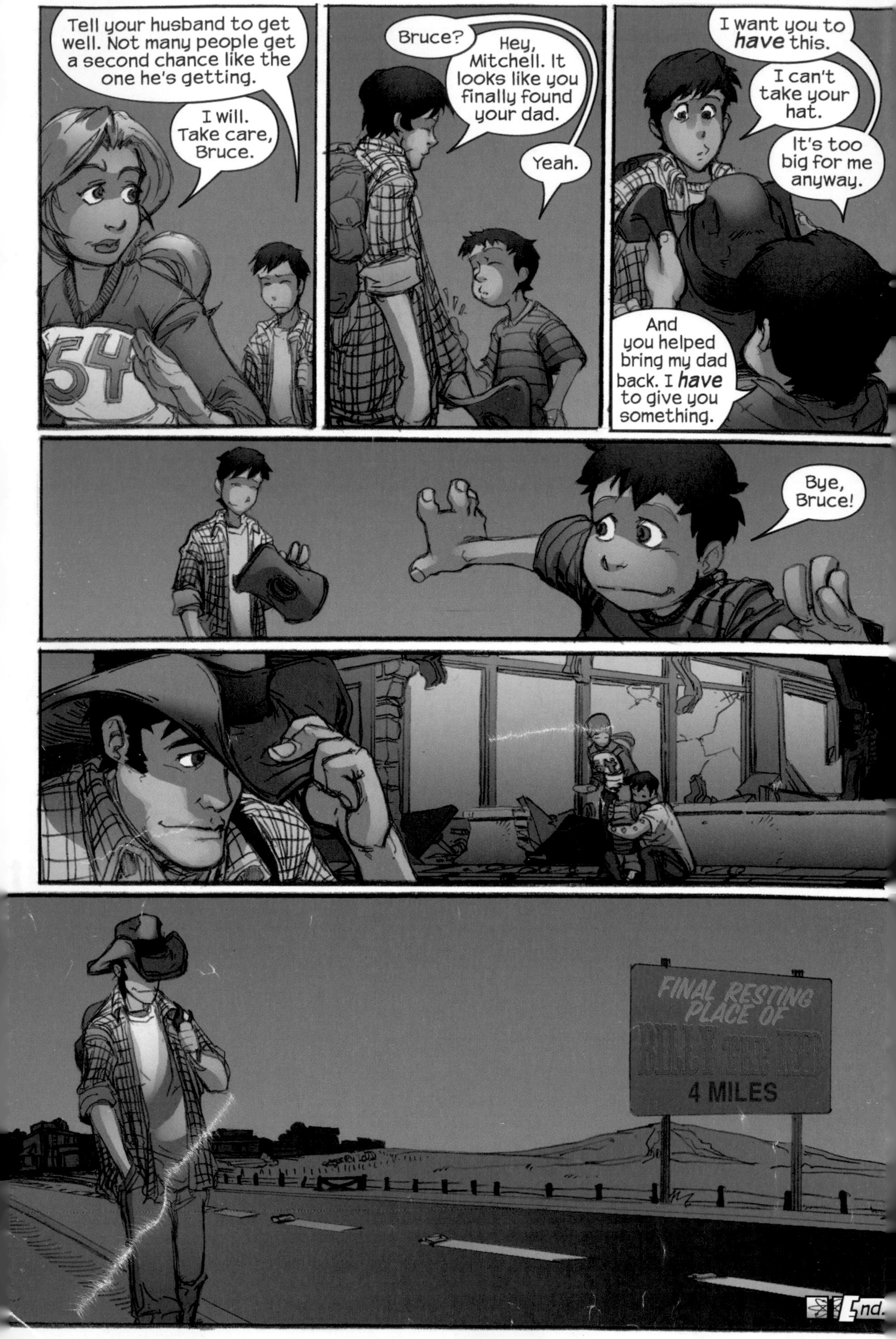

Tell your husband to get well. Not many people get a second chance like the one he's getting.
I will. Take care, Bruce.
Bruce?
Hey, Mitchell. It looks like you finally found your dad.
Yeah.
I want you to *have* this.
I can't take your hat.
It's too big for me anyway.
And you helped bring my dad back. I *have* to give you something.
Bye, Bruce!
FINAL RESTING PLACE OF
4 MILES
End.